Dear Parents:

Congratulations! Your child is tak
the first steps on an exciting jour
The destination? Independent rea

STEP INTO READING® will help your child get there. The program offers five steps to reading success. Each step includes fun stories and colorful art or photographs. In addition to original fiction and books with favorite characters, there are Step into Reading Non-Fiction Readers, Phonics Readers and Boxed Sets, Sticker Readers, and Comic Readers—a complete literacy program with something to interest every child.

Learning to Read, Step by Step!

Ready to Read   Preschool–Kindergarten
• big type and easy words • rhyme and rhythm • picture clues
For children who know the alphabet and are eager to begin reading.

Reading with Help   Preschool–Grade 1
• basic vocabulary • short sentences • simple stories
For children who recognize familiar words and sound out new words with help.

Reading on Your Own   Grades 1–3
• engaging characters • easy-to-follow plots • popular topics
For children who are ready to read on their own.

Reading Paragraphs   Grades 2–3
• challenging vocabulary • short paragraphs • exciting stories
For newly independent readers who read simple sentences with confidence.

Ready for Chapters   Grades 2–4
• chapters • longer paragraphs • full-color art
For children who want to take the plunge into chapter books but still like colorful pictures.

STEP INTO READING® is designed to give every child a successful reading experience. The grade levels are only guides; children will progress through the steps at their own speed, developing confidence in their reading. The F&P Text Level on the back cover serves as another tool to help you choose the right book for your child.

Remember, a lifetime love of reading starts with a single step!

For my nai nai
—J.H.

All rights reserved. Published in the United States by Random House Children's Books, a division of Penguin Random House LLC, New York.

Step into Reading, Random House, and the Random House colophon are registered trademarks of Penguin Random House LLC.

Visit us on the Web!
rhcbooks.com

Educators and librarians, for a variety of teaching tools, visit us at RHTeachersLibrarians.com

Library of Congress Cataloging-in-Publication Data
Name: Huang, Jackie (Paper artist), author.
Title: Grace's Chinese New Year / by Jackie Huang.
Description: First edition. | New York : Random House Children's Books, [2023] | Series: Step into reading. Step 2 | Audience: Ages 4–6. | Summary: "Grace and her family get ready to celebrate the Lunar New Year." —Provided by publisher.
Identifiers: LCCN 2022050583 (print) | LCCN 2022050584 (ebook) |
ISBN 978-0-593-57125-5 (trade paperback) | ISBN 978-0-593-57126-2 (library binding) |
ISBN 978-0-593-57127-9 (ebook)
Subjects: CYAC: Chinese New Year—Fiction. | Family life—Fiction. | LCGFT: Picture books.
Classification: LCC PZ7.1.H754 Gr 2023 (print) | LCC PZ7.1.H754 (ebook) | DDC [E]—dc23

Printed in the United States of America
10 9 8 7 6 5 4 3 2 1
First Edition

This book has been officially leveled by using the F&P Text Level Gradient™ Leveling System.

Grace's
Chinese New Year

by Jackie Huang

Random House 🏠 New York

Today is Chinese
New Year's Eve.
The holiday marks
the end of winter
and the start of spring.

It is based on the
lunar calendar.
Grace and her family
buy special food
for the celebration.

Grace and David
help clean the house.
"We must sweep away
the bad luck," says
their father.

"And make room for
the good luck, Baba,"
says Grace.

When they are done,
they make decorations
with their grandfather.

"These are blessings
for good fortune,"
says Ye Ye.
"We turn some
upside down
to invite good luck."

Next, they hang up
red lanterns.

"Why is everything red?"
Grace asks.

"Long ago in China, there was a mythical beast called Nian," says Mama.

"Nian attacked villages on New Year's Eve."

"But Nian is scared
of the color red
and loud noises!
We put up
red decorations
and light firecrackers
to scare it away!"

Something smells yummy!
Grace's grandmother is making dumplings.

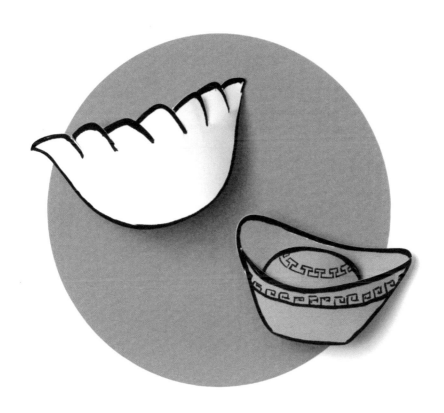

"We eat dumplings
to bring us fortune,"
says Nai Nai.
"They are the same shape
as old Chinese money."

The doorbell rings.
It's Grace's cousins,
uncles, and aunts!

noodles for *long life*

sweet rice balls
for *family*

rice cakes
for *success*

spring rolls
for *wealth*

They each bring
a special dish
for the dinner.

fish for fortune

oranges for luck

apples for peace

The elders share stories about when they lived in China.

Grace loves
hearing the stories
and having her family
together.

After dinner,
the kids say
Chinese blessings
to their aunts, uncles,
and grandparents.

Each child is given
a red envelope.
There is
lucky money inside!

Everyone says
good night.
"See you all
at the festival
tomorrow!"
says Grace.

It is finally
Chinese New Year!
Everyone dresses up
for the festival.

At the festival,
people come
from all over
to celebrate.

Soon the parade begins.
Loud drums beat and
cymbals crash.

The loud noises are
to scare away
bad spirits.

"Oh, look!" shouts David.

"It's the Lion Dance!"

The Lion Dance brings
everyone good luck
for the new year.

The night ends
with fireworks!
So pretty!

"Did you know fireworks were invented in China?" Grace tells her father. "I learned that in school."

Grace is so happy
to celebrate
Chinese New Year
with her family!